Painted Dreams

Painted Dreams

by Karen Lynn Williams

pictures by

Catherine Stock

LOTHROP, LEE & SHEPARD BOOKS · MORROW

NEW YORK

This one is for Rachel and Jonathan
— K.L.W.

Pour mes amis, Lyle et Annick
— C.S.

Watercolors were used for the full-color illustrations.
The text type is 16-point Binny Old Style.
Text copyright © 1998 by Karen Lynn Williams
Illustrations copyright © 1998 by Catherine Stock
Published by Lothrop, Lee & Shepard Books, an imprint of Morrow Junior Books, a division
of William Morrow and Company, Inc., 1350 Avenue of the Americas, New York, NY
10019, www.williammorrow.com. Printed in Singapore at Tien Wah Press.

1 2 3 4 5 6 7 8 9 10

Library of Congress Cataloging-in-Publication Data
Williams, Karen Lynn. Painted dreams/by Karen Lynn Williams;
illustrated by Catherine Stock.
p. cm.   Summary: Because her Haitian family is too poor to be able to buy paints for her,
eight-year-old Ti Marie finds her own way to create pictures that make the heart sing.
ISBN 0-688-13901-9 (trade)—ISBN 0-688-13902-7 (library) [1. Resourcefulness—
Fiction. 2. Haiti—Fiction. 3. Painting—Fiction.] I. Stock, Catherine, ill. II. Title.
PZ7.W66655Pai 1998 [E]—dc21 97-32920 CIP AC

Ti Marie sat in the early-morning shade behind her cement house and drew pictures on the rough wall. With a piece of orange brick she made a beautiful sky. With a white stone she made a giant bird, and with black charcoal she made herself, with curly dark hair.

"Ti Marie, Ti Marie. So here you are!" Mama stood over her, frowning. "I call and you don't come. You are eight years old, too old for this foolishness."

Mama bent over and rubbed out Ti Marie's picture with the hem of her dress.

"Come," she said. "I am late for market. You must watch the little ones."

Ti Marie took her sisters up the mountain to collect firewood.

"It's too hot," Josette complained.

"It's too far," Fifi whined.

The sweat trickled down Ti Marie's back, but she did not complain. Instead she dreamed about making pictures of huge green trees that would wrap the whole village in cool shade.

On their way home, the sisters passed the yard of Msie Antoine, the bocor, a powerful priest and a healer. The three houses in his compound were painted with many colorful designs that made the heart pound like a drum. A large black and red snake decorated the entrance to the biggest house. When Josette and Fifi saw it, they stopped their complaining and walked quickly past.

Ti Marie was afraid, too, but she lingered to admire the paintings. She could paint like that! With colors and brushes she could make pictures that made your heart sing.

In the afternoon Ti Marie took her sisters to the river to bathe, and they passed the home of Msie Antoine again. The bocor himself was sitting on the veranda not far from the giant snake. His back was turned to the road.

Josette and Fifi squealed and ran down the path, but not Ti Marie. Msie Antoine was painting! Holding her breath, she crept quietly up to the hedge and peeked over the barbed cactus. She could not keep her eyes from the tubes of color, the fine brushes, and the white canvas that sparkled in the sun.

Suddenly the bocor put down his brushes and turned toward the road, as though he knew someone was there. Ti Marie jumped back from the hedge and raced after her sisters.

She didn't stop to catch her breath until she reached the river.

With such fine paints, she thought as she joined her sisters in the muddy water, I would make a sparkling river racing to a blue-green sea, full of many-colored fat fish for the children to catch.

"I want to buy paints," Ti Marie told her parents as they sat by the cook fire that evening.

"Ha," her mother said. "We have no money for such things."

"But Ti Marie is a good artist," said Josette. "She makes beautiful pictures even without paints."

"One day," said Papa, "the gods will look with favor on this poor family, and I shall buy Ti Marie all the paints in the market. She will be a famous artist like Msie Antoine."

"Maybe Msie Antoine has paints for Ti Marie," said Fifi.

"You think Msie Antoine has paints to throw away on little girls?" said Mama.

Ti Marie smiled. She knew where she would get the paints.

That evening, as darkness came to the village, Ti Marie crept back to the yard of Msie Antoine. She could not see the snake in the dark—but she knew it was there.

A thin, scruffy dog was nosing through the papers and garbage outside the bocor's gate. "*Alé.* Go," Ti Marie whispered, and waved him away.

Quietly she poked at the pile, always looking over her shoulder. Her heart beat in her ears. She could barely see, but she could feel objects in the damp ashes: a rusty tin can and then a broken piece of plastic, nothing of any use. Still she raked through the heap with her fingers. There! Under a soggy piece of cardboard she found what she was looking for.

Ti Marie gathered her find up in her skirt and ran all the way home. She hid the treasure under the roots of the old mapau in the yard and slipped silently into the house.

As soon as sunlight came the next day, Ti Marie was at the mapau. She pulled the six twisted tubes of paint from their hiding place. Empty! But no, as she put them down she saw that her hands were streaked with color. She added water to the colors. Then, using chicken feathers and bunches of goat hairs as brushes, she made a small picture on a scrap of paper from the trash heap.

When Ti Marie looked up from her work, Papa was standing there. "My eldest daughter has a gift," he said. "But now you must go with your mother to the market. The little ones will come to the field with me."

The small marketplace of their village was crowded. But few people made their way back to Mama's stall at the end of the row. "No one comes to buy our fine red tomatoes and our sweet yellow onions," Mama grumbled. "The spirits have forgotten us."

Ti Marie sighed. It was true. They did not have a lucky stall. She leaned against the cool market wall. It was covered in soft green moss. Ti Marie picked at the moss with her finger. The wall underneath was smooth and white. Using a stone, she tore away the moss until she had cleaned the whole wall behind Mama's stall. It was nearly as white as Msie Antoine's canvas.

"Ti Marie!" Mama called. "It's time to go."

"Coming," she answered. She picked up her basket of vegetables. It was still full. They had sold almost nothing.

The basket was heavy, but Ti Marie did not rest until they reached the front step of their own house. Before anyone could ask her to help with chores, she dashed out back to the mapau tree and collected her paints. Then she slipped out the gate and ran back to the marketplace.

Ti Marie looked at her big clean wall for a long time. Finally, she began to paint. She used her precious colors very carefully, and when she needed them, she also used red brick, black charcoal, and bits of green moss. She used goat hairs to make fine lines and chicken feathers to make thicker ones. A hairy mango seed she found on the ground worked perfectly to fill in the large spaces with color.

Ti Marie worked as if she were in a trance until the soft light of the afternoon sun was gone.

The next morning when Ti Marie and Mama came
to the market, many people were crowded around
Mama's stall.

"What is the trouble?" Mama asked.

"No trouble," said Ti Marie. "They have come to see my pictures."

Mama looked at the leafy green trees with many-colored birds in their branches and the huge chicken and fat pig, each big enough to feed a whole village. Then she reached out a finger to trace the tiny market girl with a giant basket full of fine red tomatoes the size of soccer balls and golden yellow onions as big as the sun.

Without a word, she quickly put out her tomatoes and onions. Ti Marie helped to make neat piles.

It seemed as if the entire village came to admire Ti Marie's paintings, and while they were there, people bought Mama's fine vegetables.

Even Papa and Josette and Fifi came.
"In the gardens, people are talking of Ti Marie's paintings," Papa said.

Mama nodded. "It's like carnival. So many customers. We barely have enough room here."

"Look!" squeaked Josette.

Wide-eyed with fear, Fifi just pointed.

Msie Antoine was standing in front of the pictures. He looked at them a long time. Finally he turned to Mama.

"Who has done this work?" he asked.

"My eldest daughter, Msie," she said quietly.

The bocor looked straight at Ti Marie. "You have a gift from the spirits. You should practice this talent." His smile was warm and friendly.

Ti Marie could only smile back. Yes, she would practice, for there were many more pictures she wanted to make. Ti Marie stood beside Msie Antoine in the stall at the end of the marketplace and looked at all the people who had come to see her paintings. She knew she could not dream a better picture than this.

Author's Note

Living for two years in Deschapelles, Haiti, I was impressed by the number of Haitians who are artists. Their varied and colorful works articulate a joy and dignity that transcend the daily hardships of life in the poorest country in the Western Hemisphere. Haiti's history has been one of constant political turmoil and economic instability. It has always been difficult for artists to obtain paints, brushes, and canvas. But Haitian artists always seem to find a way to create art. It is not unusual to come upon houses in the countryside with brilliantly painted walls, or, in urban areas, to see trucks, vans, and buses called taptaps decorated with great imagination.

Haitian paintings are characterized by the use of bright colors, naive perspective, large shapes, and minute details. Dreams and surrealistic fantasies are favorite subjects, often featuring foods of unbelievable proportions, lush landscapes, village scenes, and jungle animals. Painters may borrow characters and stories from African and European folklore for subject matter. Humor and political satire are also common themes.

Many Haitian artists begin their craft at an early age. They come from various backgrounds and are often self-taught, with little or no formal schooling. One of Haiti's most famous artists, Hyppolite, was a voodoo priest—as Msie Antoine, in this story, is. In the past, most Haitian artists have been men, but now the number of female artists is growing.

Glossary of Creole Words

Alé (ah-LEH): Contraction of the French verb *aller,* "to go"

Bocor (BOH-coor): A voodoo priest

Mapau (Mah-PAHOH): A flowering tree

Msie (Mih-SEE-ah): Contraction of *monsieur,* the French word for "mister"

Ti (Tee): Contraction of *petite,* the French word for "little"